To Michael, David, and Chrissy—who love to wreak
havoc while Mom and Dad snore on
—K. W.

For Alan Baker, my tutor
—J. C.

Margaret K. McElderry Books
An imprint of Simon & Schuster Children's Publishing
1230 Avenue of the Americas
New York, NY 10020

Book design by Ann Bobco
The text of this book is set in Adobe Caslon.
The illustrations were rendered in acrylic paint.

Printed in Hong Kong

12 14 16 18 20 19 17 15 13

Library of Congress Cataloging-in-Publication Data
Wilson, Karma.
Bear snores on / Karma Wilson ; illustrations by Jane Chapman. -- 1st ed.
p. cm.
Summary: On a cold winter night many animals gather to party in the cave of a sleeping bear,
who then awakes and protests that he has missed the food and the fun.
ISBN 0-689-83187-0
[1. Bears--Fiction. 2. Animals--Fiction. 3. Parties--Fiction. 4. Stories in rhyme.] I. Chapman, Jane, 1970- ill. II. Title.

PZ8.3.W6976 Be 2001
[E]--dc21
00-028371

Bear Snores On

From: Valerie + Aunt Angela 2015

Karma Wilson

illustrations by Jane Chapman

MARGARET K. MCELDERRY BOOKS

New York   London   Toronto   Sydney   Singapore

*I*n a cave in the woods,
in his deep, dark lair,
through the long, cold winter
sleeps a great brown bear.

Cuddled in a heap,
with his eyes shut tight,
he sleeps through the day,
he sleeps through the night.

The cold winds howl
and the night sounds growl.

But
the bear
snores on.

An itty-bitty mouse,
pitter-pat, tip-toe,
creep-crawls in the cave
from the fluff-cold snow.

Mouse squeaks, "Too damp,
too dank, too dark."
So he lights wee twigs
with a small, hot spark.

The coals pip-pop and the wind doesn't stop.

But
the bear
snores on.

Two glowing eyes
sneak-peek in the den.
Mouse cries, "Who's there?"
and a hare hops in.

"Ho, Mouse!" says Hare.
"Long time, no see!"
So they pop white corn.
And they brew black tea.

Mouse sips wee slurps.
Hare burps big BURPS!

But
the bear
snores on.

A badger scuttles by,
sniff-snuffs at the air.
"I smell yummy-yums!
Perhaps we can share?

"I've brought honey-nuts,"
Badger says with a grin.
"Let's divvy them up,
cozy down . . . and dig in!"

And they nibble and they munch with a

CHEW–

CHOMP–

CRUNCH!

But
the bear
snores on.

A gopher and a mole
tunnel up through the floor.
Then a wren and a raven
flutter in through the door!

Mole mutters, "What a night!"
"What a storm!" twitters Wren.
And everybody clutters
in the great bear's den.

They tweet and they titter. They chat and they chitter.

But
the bear
snores on.

*I*n a cave in the woods,
a slumbering bear
sleeps through the party
in his very own lair.

Hare stokes the fire.
Mouse seasons stew.

Then a small pepper fleck
makes the bear . . . .

R A A A A A - C H O O

He blows and he sneezes,
and the whole crowd freezes . . .

And
the bear
WAKES UP!

BEAR GNARLS

and he SNARLS.

BEAR ROARS

and he RUMBLES!

BEAR JUMPS

and he STOMPS.

BEAR GROWLS

and he GRUMBLES!

"You've snuck in my lair
and you've all had fun!
But me? I was sleeping
and . . .

I have had none!"

And he whimpers
and he moans,
he wails and he groans . . .

And the bear blubbers on!

Mouse squeaks, "Don't fret.
Don't fuss. Look, see?
We can pop more corn!
We can brew more tea!"

Bear gulps. Bear gobbles.
He sighs with delight.
Then he spins tall tales
through the blustery night.

When the sun peeks up
on a crisp, clear dawn,
Bear can't sleep . . .

But
his friends
snore on.